Licensed exclusively to Top That Publishing Ltd
Tide Mill Way, Woodbridge, Suffolk, IP12 1AP, UK
www.topthatpublishing.com
Copyright © 2014 Tide Mill Media
All rights reserved
2 4 6 8 9 7 5 3
Manufactured in China

Written by Robert Louis Stevenson
Illustrated by Sara Sanchez

ISBN 978-1-78244-913-3

A catalogue record for this book is available from the British Library

My Shadow

by Robert Louis Stevenson

I have a little shadow
that goes **in** and **out** with me,

And what can be the use
of him is more than I can see.

He is very, very like me
from the heels

up to the head;

And I see him **jump** before me,

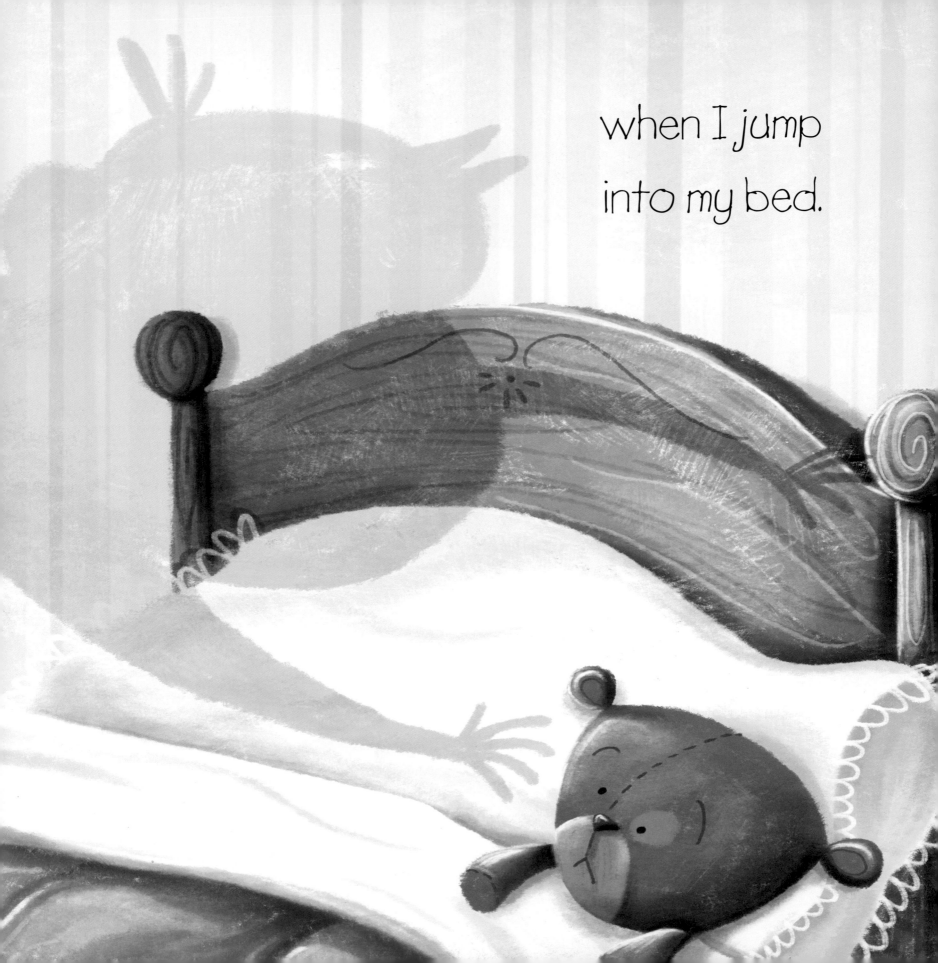

when I jump
into my bed.

The funniest thing about him is the way he likes to grow.

Not at all like
proper children,
which is always very
slow;

For he sometimes shoots up

like a bouncy rubber ball,

And he sometimes gets so little
that there's none of him at all.

He hasn't got a notion of how
children ought to play,

And can only make a fool of me
in every sort of way.

He stays so close beside me,

he's a **coward**, you can see;

I'm too brave to stick to mummy as
that shadow **sticks** to me!

One morning, very early,
before the sun was up,

I rose and found the shining
dew on every buttercup;

But my lazy
little shadow,
like a naughty
sleepy-head.

Had stayed at home behind me
and was fast asleep in bed.

The End